REACH THEIR GOAL!

Tristan Howard

A
LITTLE **APPLE**
PAPERBACK

SCHOLASTIC INC.
New York Toronto London Auckland Sydney

No part of this publication may be reproduced in whole or in part, or stored in a retrieval system, or transmitted in any form or by any means, electronic, mechanical, photocopying, recording, or otherwise, without written permission of the publisher. For information regarding permission, write to Scholastic Inc., 555 Broadway, New York, NY 10012.

ISBN 0-590-92133-9

Produced by Daniel Weiss Associates, Inc.
33 West 17th Street, New York, NY 10011

12 11 10 9 8 7 6 5 4 3 2 1   6 7 8 9/9 0 1/0

Printed in the U.S.A.   40

First Scholastic printing, October 1996

Chapter 1

"I got it!"

Brenda Bailey kicked the soccer ball as hard as she could. It sailed down to the other end of the field. "Yeah!" Brenda yelled. She pumped her fist in the air. "Hurry, Adam!"

Adam Fingerhut ran slowly toward the ball. Adam isn't a very good soccer player. He looks like he thinks the ball might explode if he gets too close. "Go, Adam!" I shouted. I cupped my hands around my mouth

1

so that he could hear me. "Kick the ball!"

Adam stopped the ball with his foot. Then he turned around and kicked it. I groaned. It would be an easy play for the other team's goalie.

"I got it!" the goalie yelled. She reached out to pick up the ball.

"No, I got it!" It was Mitchell Rubin's voice. I rubbed my eyes. Where had Mitchell come from? He must have run like lightning to get to the goal so quickly! "Yay, Mitchell!" I yelled.

Mitchell kicked the ball before the goalie could grab it. "Get it, Catherine!" he shouted.

That was me! I took a deep breath and stopped the ball. Then I looked to see what I could do. The goalie was blocking my way, so instead I kicked it to my teammate Joanna Wrightman. Joanna was running hard, too. She took careful aim—and kicked it right into the net.

The referee blew her whistle. "Goal!" she shouted.

"Great shot, Joanna!" I called out.

But Mitchell and Joanna kept running. "Help!" Joanna cried as they whizzed past the goalie.

Wham! They landed in the back of the net, right next to the ball.

"Are you all right?" I asked, hurrying to see.

Joanna laughed. "Just fine," she said. "If I can get out of the net again, that is!" She started to stand up, but she tripped over a rope and fell back to the ground.

"It's harder than it looks," Mitchell said. His whole body was covered in string. "Maybe this is the way out."

3

He pulled on a loose part of the net and started to wriggle.

"I think you'll just get more stuck that way," I said.

Mitchell's shoe popped off. "Oh, that's okay," he said. "I'll pretend I'm a fly and I got caught by a spider."

Joanna's eyes lit up. "I'll be the spider," she said. She pretended to climb along the bottom of the rope. "Yum, yum! Fresh bug!" she said in a silly voice.

I forgot all about the soccer game. "I'll play, too," I said, and jumped into the middle of the goal. My arm went through a hole in the net. "Can I be another fly?"

"I think I'll be a cricket instead," Mitchell said. "An alien cricket." He made chirping noises in a robot voice.

"Catherine! Mitchell! Joanna! Are you all right?"

I looked up with a start. My mother was standing over us. She coaches our soccer team, and she was frowning. "Can't you get out?" she asked.

I turned red. "Yeah," I said. I moved my arm to show that I could get out. Only it caught on something. I turned this way and that, trying to find the hole I'd stuck my arm through.

But it wasn't anywhere.

Rats. Now I was *really* stuck.

"We're just playing, Mrs. Antler," Joanna said. She smiled at my mom. "See, we're caught in the spiderweb, and—"

"An *alien* spiderweb," Mitchell corrected her.

"Yeah, an alien spiderweb," Joanna agreed. "I'm the alien spider. See my powerful antennae?" She wiggled her braids back and forth.

"And her poisonous fangs," Mitchell put in.

Joanna made a horrible face. "Fun, huh?"

Mom shook her head. "You kids are silly," she told us. "But we need to get on with the game. See, everyone's waiting."

 "Oops," Mitchell said with a grin.

"Joanna!" Joanna's father, Mr. Wrightman, appeared next to the goal. The Wrightmans had just moved to Maplewood. "The next time you get the ball, make sure you kick with the inside of your foot, all right? And try to dribble to the goalie's left before you shoot."

"Sure, Dad," Joanna said cheerfully. She wriggled out of the net. So did Mitchell. Together they ran back to the field.

I struggled to get loose, too. But the next thing I knew, a loop of net was stuck tightly around my ankle.

Mr. Wrightman shook his head and sighed. "Sometimes I wish Joanna would take sports a little more seriously," he said.

"It sounds as if you know a lot about soccer, Mr. Wrightman," Mom said.

Mr. Wrightman smiled. "I used to play when I was in college," he told her.

Mom looked like she was about to say something. Then she noticed me, still tangled up in the goal. "Catherine?" she asked curiously.

"I'm trying to get out, Mom," I said. "But I think I'm stuck tight." I wriggled around one of the goalposts. It didn't seem to help.

"Oh, dear." Mom picked up one of the ropes. "Maybe if you go under this one?"

I tried. No luck. Now I couldn't move my hand at all.

Mr. Wrightman rolled his eyes. "I guess Joanna's not the only one," he said.

"I'm sorry," I said.

Mr. Wrightman found the hole I'd been looking for. He pushed me through it. I landed with a thump. "Thanks, Mr. Wrightman," I said, rubbing the dirt off my legs.

Mr. Wrightman gave me a grin. "You're welcome, Catherine," he said. "Listen, next time think about what you're going to do with the ball before you get it, all right? That's what real soccer players do."

I nodded. But I wasn't sure if I could or not. Mr. Wrightman's suggestion sounded awfully hard.

"And Catherine," Mr. Wrightman went on, "a soccer net is an important piece of equipment. It's not a toy. Okay?"

I hung my head. "Okay." I stood up and ran back to my team.

Our soccer team is called the Rangers, but sometimes we like to call ourselves the Leftovers. We're the players none of the other teams wanted. Sometimes you can understand why. Josh Ramos kicks the ball so hard it usually rolls out of bounds. Mitchell says he gets messages from aliens— through his shoes! And Lucy Marcus spends most of her practice time balancing on a soccer ball. We're all in second or third grade, and my mom is the coach, even though she doesn't know anything about soccer.

Matt Carter gave me a funny look when I got back to my position. "Were you really stuck?" he asked. "Or were you just pretending?"

"I was really stuck," I told him. The other team kicked off.

"Oh," Matt said. "Mitchell said it was a spiderweb. Was it sticky?"

"No," I said. "Look, here comes the ball."

Matt didn't notice. "You should always carry a pair of scissors in case you get trapped in a spiderweb," he told me. "Then you'll be safe, no matter what."

"The ball, Matt!" I said, pointing. "Get the ball!"

Matt still didn't turn around. "And besides—" he began.

Wham!

The ball hit Matt right in the back and knocked him over. "Ow!" he yelled as he hit the ground. He lay perfectly still.

"Get the ball, Matt!" Mom called. But I heard another voice from near the bench, louder and higher than Mom's. It was Lucy Marcus's little sister, Ava.

"Matt *dead*!" she shouted joyfully.

Matt raised his head and started to laugh.

And the rest of us began to crack up, too.

Chapter 2

We won the game, 5–4. After the game was over, we lined up for Popsicles.

Adam pushed his way in front of Josh. I was surprised when Josh didn't push back. But Josh just smiled. "First is the worst," he reminded Adam. "Second is the best." He pointed to himself.

"Hey!" Adam said. "I'm not the worst!"

Josh pointed to Adam. "First is the worst," he repeated. "Second is the best." Then he touched Brenda, who was standing behind him. "And third is the one with the treasure chest."

"That's me," Brenda said happily. "I got a treasure chest," she sang. "I got a treasure chest."

"I thought it was 'Third is the one who forgot to get dressed,'" Mitchell said in a robot voice. Everybody laughed.

"Here you go, Adam," Mom said. She handed him a grape Popsicle.

"You can have it, Josh," Adam said, trying to duck behind Josh.

"No way!" Josh backed up so Adam couldn't squeeze in. He banged into Brenda, who banged into Matt, who banged into Lucy, who banged against a tree. "Hey!" Lucy shouted.

Mom sighed. "Come on, Adam," she said.

Adam shook his head. "I'd rather not have a Popsicle at all," he said.

"Josh can be the worst." He sat down and folded his arms.

"Then Brenda would be the best," Matt said, counting. "And I'd be the one with the treasure chest."

"Fourth is the king," I said, pointing to Lucy. "And fifth is the queen." Fifth was Julie Zimmer. That made sense. Julie cares a lot about how she looks. Even after a whole soccer game, she didn't have a speck of dirt on her—anywhere!

"I don't want to be the king," Lucy complained. "I'd rather be a cowgirl." She pretended to ride a horse. "Let's make it 'Fourth is the cowgirl, fifth is the queen.'"

"And sixth is the one in the washing machine!" I said, pointing to Alex Slavik.

"He *should* go in the washing machine!" Matt said.

Alex isn't very good at sports. He

falls down a lot. Sometimes he trips over the ball. More often he trips over his own feet. I agreed with Matt. Alex looked like he was ready for the washing machine, all right.

"If Lucy's out of line, I don't want a Popsicle, either," said Alex. "I don't want to be the queen."

"Then I'll be queen," Yin Wong said loudly. She pushed in front of Alex.

"Isn't anybody hungry?" Mom held out the grape Popsicle. "Should I eat it myself?"

We all looked at each other. All of us were hungry. And thirsty. In soccer you run around a lot. You try to kick the ball into the other team's goal, and you can get very thirsty in a hurry!

But none of us wanted to be first. Not after Josh told us that first was the worst.

"Matt not dead?" Lucy's sister Ava asked. She stared up at Matt.

Matt's big sister Sara stroked Ava's forehead. She usually takes care of Ava during our games. "Matt's still alive," she said. "For now! But if he doesn't stop fooling with my stuff—"

Mr. Wrightman didn't let her finish. "I don't understand why you kids can't just line up and eat your Popsicles," he said, scratching his head.

I made a face at Lucy. It was just the kind of thing a grown-up would say.

"And by the way, you kids should try harder to concentrate," Mr. Wrightman went on. "The other team scored a few goals that they shouldn't have scored. A real soccer player pays attention. All the time!"

Mom nodded. "Mr. Wrightman, I've been meaning to ask you—" she began.

But Josh interrupted. "All right," he said. "I'll be first. Adam can be after me."

"Yay!" Adam cheered. "I'm the

best!" He squeezed in front of Brenda.

"But Josh," Danny West said, "do you really want to be . . . you know what?"

I knew what he was thinking: Did Josh really want to be the worst?

Josh grinned and took his Popsicle. "I'm not first," he said. "I'm zero. Zero comes before first. And zero is the hero."

"But—" Adam began.

"That means you're first, Adam," Lucy said. "And Brenda is the best. And Matt gets to be the one with the treasure chest." She sounded disappointed.

"You can have my place, Lucy," Matt offered. "I'd rather be the king."

Adam bit his lip. "I'll be another zero," he said. "Double zero. That makes me a double hero." But no one was listening.

We all got our Popsicles, even

though we moved around to do it. Julie got to be the queen. Yin was the one in the washing machine. I was number eight, so I was the one who was always late.

That was okay. It was better than Joanna, who was ninth. "Nine is the one who was wasting time," Josh called when it was her turn.

"Mr. Wrightman, could I see you for a moment?" Mom asked when all the Popsicles had been handed out. They walked to the other side of the bench.

Danny West finished his Popsicle first. "Zero!" he yelled out. "Zero is the hero!" He showed everyone his empty stick. "Zero's the hero—that's me!"

No one wanted to finish next. That person would be "first is the worst." So we tried very hard to lick as slowly as we could.

"Come on, Matt," Lucy said. "Let's do somersaults."

I was about to ask Mitchell and Joanna if alien spiders had claws. But suddenly Mom clapped her hands. "Quiet, please," she said. "I have an announcement."

"What, Mrs. Antler?" Danny asked. "Is it football season now?"

"Do we get seconds on Popsicles?" Brenda wanted to know.

Matt poked me. "Did we win today, or did we lose?" he whispered. "I forgot."

Mr. Wrightman stood next to Mom. "I'm going to be stepping down," Mom said.

"Stepping down?" Alex looked blank. "Where? Where are the stairs?"

"Stepping down means I won't be coach anymore," Mom explained. "Mr. Wrightman is taking over. He knows a lot about soccer. And it will help the Wrightmans feel more at home here in Maplewood."

"That's right." Mr. Wrightman

nodded. "I'll see you here tomorrow afternoon for practice. Be on time!"

I stared at Mom. She doesn't know much about soccer, I told myself. And Mr. Wrightman knows a lot.

Still, it was hard to imagine somebody else coaching us.

Chapter 3

"Hey, Matt!" Lucy shouted. It was almost time for soccer practice the next day. "Want to hear a riddle?"

"Sure!" Matt was digging a hole near the goalposts.

Lucy grinned. "Why was six afraid of seven?" she asked.

I scratched my head. "Because seven was bigger?" I guessed.

"Uh-uh," Lucy said with a giggle. "Try again."

"Seven is perfect, eight is the same,"

Matt chanted. "But nine is the one with the hairy brain."

"Oh, that's not how it goes," I told him. "It's '*Ten* is perfect, *eleven* is the same.'" Maybe next time I'd try to be the tenth person in line.

Or the eleventh.

"That isn't the answer anyway," Lucy told us. "Give up?"

I looked around the field to see if I could get an idea. Joanna and Brenda were making snow angels in the grass—even though there wasn't any snow! Josh and Adam were having a race. Josh was winning. And Mitchell and Yin were playing follow-the-leader on the white out-of-bounds line.

I shook my head. "I give up."

"Because—" Lucy began.

Suddenly someone blew a whistle so loudly I wanted to cover my ears. I looked around.

"Oh, it's just Mr. Wrightman," Lucy said, rolling her eyes.

"Mr. Wrightman, Mr. Wrightman," Matt said in a silly voice. He lay down and peered into the hole he'd dug. "Mr. Wrightman is the Wrongman," he said.

"He sure can blow that whistle," Lucy said.

"Team!" Mr. Wrightman was waving to us. "Now!"

We all walked over and stood near Mr. Wrightman. "Sit down, kids," he told us. But no one sat down.

"Remember, first is the worst," Matt whispered to me.

I watched Adam and Josh to see if they would sit down. I wanted to be second. Or maybe I'd wait till number ten or number eleven, because being perfect would be good, too.

But I didn't want to be the worst. Or the one with the hairy brain.

23

Mr. Wrightman frowned. "Please sit down now," he said in a stern voice.

We all tumbled to the ground.

"I was third," Matt whispered. "I get the treasure chest."

"If you want to be good at soccer, you need to work at it," Mr. Wrightman said. "I can teach you lots of stuff, but you have to practice. Practice, practice, practice—that's what soccer's all about. Today we'll start with lots of drills."

Matt and I frowned at each other. That sounded kind of boring.

"I know you can play better than you did yesterday," Mr. Wrightman went on.

Danny raised his hand. "But Mr. Wrightman, we won."

"Yes," Mr. Wrightman agreed. "But you won by only one point. I can teach you to play well enough to win by ten points."

"Why would we want to win by ten points?" Julie asked.

"The other team wouldn't like that," Danny said.

"Close games are more exciting," Brenda put in. "Winning by lots isn't fun."

"Fun?" Mr. Wrightman looked surprised. "Who said soccer was supposed to be fun? Let's do some running. Take five laps around the field. Go!"

"Laps? That reminds me of a riddle," Matt said. "What do you lose whenever you stand up?"

"Carter!" Mr. Wrightman pointed a finger at Matt. "Don't talk! Just run!"

"You lose your lap," Matt hissed to me. "Get it?"

I got it, and I would have laughed. But Mr. Wrightman grabbed his whistle and blew a long blast. Everybody froze. This time I did put my hands over my ears.

"I said no talking!" Mr. Wrightman said. "Go! Now!"

When we were done, I collapsed under a tree. I was out of breath. "Can we kick the ball now?" Danny asked.

"Yeah!" Joanna sat up and grinned at her father. "How about a practice game?"

Mr. Wrightman shook his head. "We have things to work on," he said. "And no talking during practice!"

Instead of a practice game, we did lots of exercises—stretching exercises, sit-ups, jumping jacks. And if we tried to talk, Mr. Wrightman made us run extra laps.

It happened a lot. Especially to Matt.

At last Mr. Wrightman stopped the exercises. He put us around the field and gave Mitchell a soccer ball. "Pass it so everyone gets a chance," he told us.

"Like this?" Mitchell started to kick it to Adam.

Tweet, tweet, tweet! Mr. Wrightman held up his hand. "Not yet!" he said. He sounded annoyed. "The last person shoots it into the goal. Try to do it in less than one minute. Go!"

One minute? I thought. With people like Alex on our team, there was no way we could do it that fast.

In fact, we never even got the ball to Alex. Mitchell kicked it to Adam, who kicked it to Danny, who kicked it to Julie, who got confused and passed it back to Mitchell. Mr. Wrightman just shook his head.

When we tried again, Danny kicked it too hard and Yin couldn't get it. Mr. Wrightman sighed. Then Lucy forgot who was next. Mr. Wrightman rolled his eyes.

After ten tries, we still hadn't gotten the ball anywhere near the goal. And Mr. Wrightman was getting red in the face.

"What's so hard about this?" he asked. He sounded confused. "First one person kicks it. Then the next. Then the next. It's easy! Real soccer players can do it with their eyes closed."

But we're not real soccer players, I thought. We're just kids!

Mr. Wrightman took a deep breath. "Everybody run around the field three more times. Maybe that will wake you up. Go!"

We all ran. When we were done, our faces were as red as Mr. Wrightman's.

"Mr. Wrightman?" Julie panted. "I'm tired. Can't we go home?"

"Yeah," Josh added. "This isn't any fun."

"But kids—" Mr. Wrightman looked unhappy. "I'm sure you can score a goal in less than a minute if you just try a little harder."

"I don't think we'll ever do it that fast, Mr. Wrightman," Mitchell said sadly.

"Maybe when we're fourteen years old," Matt added. "Or thirty-five."

Mr. Wrightman sighed. "All right," he said. "Go home. But come back tomorrow—ready to work!"

Work? I thought. What does he think we've just been doing?

Lucy and I walked home very slowly. Our whole bodies felt sore. Even our bones hurt.

"You never answered your riddle," I reminded her. "Why was six afraid of seven?"

"Because seven ate nine," Lucy said. "Get it?"

"I get it," I said. Seven *ate* nine. Seven *eight* nine.

It was pretty funny.

But I was too worn out to laugh.

Chapter 4

"What are you doing, Alex?" I asked.

It was just before practice the next day. Alex was down on his hands and knees in front of one of the goals.

"Building," Alex told me.

"Building?" I asked. "On a soccer field?"

"Yeah," Alex said. "I was figuring out a way to keep the ball out of the goal." Alex is usually our goalie. "Mr. Wrightman won't like it if I let in any goals tomorrow."

I nodded. Alex was probably right.

"So I'm building a wall," Alex explained. "Out of dirt and rocks. The ball will hit it and bounce back. See?"

He was pointing at a tiny pile of dirt. It was maybe as tall as my fingernail. I couldn't imagine how it would stop a soccer ball. "Is it big enough?" I asked.

"I think so," Alex said. "I didn't want to make it taller because I don't want the referee to see it."

"Oh," I said. "That makes sense."

Tweet! Mr. Wrightman blew his whistle. "Eight laps!" he ordered.

I groaned. But I started to run. And so did Alex. Everything was fine until the fifth lap. We were just crossing the goal line when *boom*—Alex's legs flew out from under him and he landed on his side.

"Ow!" he yelled.

"Are you all right?" I asked.

"Yeah," he said, rubbing his ribs. "I guess I tripped over my wall."

I looked down at the tiny wall Alex had built and shook my head. Only an ant could trip over a wall that small, I thought.

Only an ant—or Alex!

We did get to play a practice game later on. After we'd finished all our sit-ups and jumping jacks, of course. But the practice game wasn't a lot of fun.

It's not much fun when your coach keeps rolling his eyes.

"Marcus!" Mr. Wrightman called to Lucy one time. "Stop doing cartwheels and kick the ball!"

Lucy bit her lip and stared at the ground.

"But Mr. Wrightman," Danny said. He pulled at Mr. Wrightman's sleeve. "You can't tell Lucy not to do cartwheels."

"Yeah," Matt said. "That would be like telling the sun not to rise every morning."

"She can do cartwheels whenever she wants," Mr. Wrightman told them. He put his hands on his hips. "But not during a game! How can this team win with a player doing cartwheels on the field?"

Another time, Brenda kicked the ball toward the white line at the edge of the field. When she saw that the ball would roll out of bounds, she stopped chasing it.

Mr. Wrightman sighed loudly. "Bailey! Hustle!"

Brenda looked miserable. I was surprised, because usually when Brenda's on a soccer field, she's grinning.

"It was going out of bounds," Joanna explained. "Brenda couldn't get there in time."

"Yeah, she doesn't have a rocket engine on her back," Mitchell said.

"Always run on a soccer field!" Mr. Wrightman pounded his fist into the palm of his other hand. *"Always!"*

* * *

The next day wasn't any better. After lots and lots of laps and exercises, we played another practice game. Only we kept stopping.

When Adam kicked the ball with his toe instead of the side of his foot, Mr. Wrightman made everyone sit down while he showed Adam how to do it right. He was with Adam for five whole minutes. But at the end Adam was still kicking the ball off his toe. And Mr. Wrightman didn't look happy.

"Why is he upset?" I whispered to Julie. "Adam *always* kicks the ball with his toe. He'll do it right when he's ready."

The next time the ball came near Adam, he just let it roll by.

When Yin threw the ball in from out of bounds, Mr. Wrightman stopped the

Throw In

game again to show her how to do it right. Yin tried over and over, but she couldn't please Mr. Wrightman.

The next time the ball went out of bounds, Mr. Wrightman asked Yin to throw it in. But Yin just shook her head.

At last Mr. Wrightman stopped the game to show Alex how to kick the ball without falling down.

I flopped down next to Lucy. "This will take a while," I said.

"Maybe a few years," Lucy said. She grinned. "Maybe a few centuries."

"Not like that!" Mr. Wrightman sounded frustrated.

I looked at Alex's face. He looked more confused than ever. Poor Alex.

"Look!" Josh lay down with his hands flat on the ground. Then he pushed his bottom up in the air so that he looked like a crab. "I can do the crab walk!" He took a few steps. Then he fell down, laughing.

"I can do that, too," Julie said. "Let's all do it."

It looked like fun, and it was easy to get into the crab position. What wasn't so easy was staying up! "I'll race you, Adam," I said as Adam crashed to the ground.

"No." Brenda's eyes lit up. "Let's play soccer this way!"

"Crab soccer!" Lucy cheered. "Yeah, let's!"

Mitchell threw a ball to us. We started skittering around the field, trying to get it. It was hard work. But it was fun.

"I got it!" Josh gave the ball a big kick. Then he toppled over. The ball rolled to me. I closed my eyes and kicked with all my might.

Brenda got the ball and started dribbling toward the goal. Matt scurried over to block her. I turned around and bumped heads with Danny. "Hey, this is fun!" Danny said. He grinned at me.

"Maybe we should play in a crab soccer league instead."

"Bren-da! Bren-da!" Mitchell was chanting, and Yin joined in: "Bren-da! Bren-da!" Brenda was almost to the goal. But at the last minute Adam kicked out his leg and knocked the ball away from her.

"Yay, Adam!" I yelled. I didn't know if he was on my team or not, but it was a good play. Everyone was grinning. Everyone was having a good time.

"Get it, Catherine!" Julie shouted as she kicked the ball down the field. I moved toward it. My legs were swaying like crazy. I was almost there when—

Tweeeeeeeeeeeet!

Everybody froze. I don't think anybody even breathed.

We all knew who was blowing that whistle.

And we all guessed he wasn't going to like what we were doing.

Chapter 5

"Mom?" I asked the next day. We were driving to our game against the Angels. "How come you quit being our coach?"

Mom looked surprised. "Because Mr. Wrightman knows a lot about soccer," she said. "Don't you think a soccer coach should be good at soccer?"

"Yeah," I admitted. "But . . ." I tried to find the right words. "Just knowing about soccer doesn't make you a good coach."

"No?" Mom raised her eyebrows. "What do you mean?"

I thought about how Mr. Wrightman wanted us to do everything perfectly—even though we're only seven and eight years old. How he had growled at Alex for falling down. And made Matt run extra laps for talking. And gotten mad when we played crab soccer during practice. I sighed.

"Oh, nothing," I said.

The Angels were already on the field when we got there. They were running, yelling, and throwing grass. Every now and then they would kick the ball. They weren't very good. But they were having fun.

Then I looked at our team.

Everybody was in a circle. Even Lucy. Matt was standing perfectly straight. They were all listening to Mr. Wrightman. And they all looked pretty unhappy.

"We can beat these kids," Mr. Wrightman was saying as I ran up. He stamped his foot on the ground. "We can crush them. We can pulverize them."

"What does that mean?" Alex asked.

Mr. Wrightman didn't answer him. "What are you going to do out there?"

We looked at each other. But no one said a word.

Mr. Wrightman rolled his eyes. "I said, what are you going to do out there?" he asked again.

Brenda raised her hand timidly. "Play hard?" she asked.

"Play well," Danny suggested.

"Kick lots of goals," Julie put in.

Mr. Wrightman waved his hand in the air. "And what's most important of all?"

"Teamwork?" Matt asked shyly.

I thought back to what Mom had always told us before a game. She'd always said to play hard. And to be safe. And—

"Have fun!" I cried out.

"Yeah!" Mitchell clapped me on the back. Suddenly everyone was smiling. "Let's have fun!" Josh shouted. He put his hand into the middle of the circle, the way Mom always did. Brenda and Joanna put their hands on top of his.

"Go, Rangers!" we started to shout—

Go Rangers!!

Tweet! Tweet! Tweet!

Everyone froze.

"Having fun is nice," Mr. Wrightman said. His eyes flashed. "But winning is the most important thing of all!"

"Win," Yin echoed in a very small voice.

Adam gulped. "Yeah. Let's win." But he didn't say it like he meant it.

"*Now* it's time for 'Go, Rangers,'" Mr. Wrightman said. He put his hand in the middle. "Well? What are you waiting for?"

Slowly we put our hands in the circle. "Go, Rangers," we said.

The game started off pretty well. Josh scored a goal, and we cheered. Then Joanna kicked a goal, too, and so did Mitchell. We were leading, 3–0.

But Mr. Wrightman wasn't very happy. Every time we had the ball and didn't score, he would call us over to explain what we'd done wrong. If we didn't kick a perfect pass, he would shake his head. He even complained when Mitchell scored his goal.

"Kick faster!" he told Mitchell. "Real soccer players don't wait that long!"

Just before halftime, one of the Angels stole the ball. He dribbled it past Adam and around Danny. Then he fired.

Whoosh!

The ball went past Alex and into the net.

But we were still ahead, 3–1. When the whistle blew, we were feeling pretty good. We went to the bench for some water and apple slices.

"First is the worst!" yelled Julie. She squeezed in line behind Mitchell.

"I'm the hero," Mitchell reminded her. "Zero is the hero, remember?"

"I don't want to be eight," Brenda said. "I think I'll be seven and a half instead. That's how old I really am. What do I get to be then?"

Danny thought. "Seven and a half didn't ever take a bath," he said.

"That doesn't rhyme," Joanna pointed out. "How about 'Seven and a half got to sit down and laugh'?"

"Okay." Brenda grinned. "They both sound good."

"Aren't we playing well, Mr. Wrightman?" Julie asked proudly.

Mr. Wrightman shook his head. "I'm disappointed," he said sadly. "I expected more than this."

Mitchell stared at Mr. Wrightman. "But we're winning," he said. "We're winning by two whole goals!"

"Who likes Popsicles after the game?" Mr. Wrightman asked.

We all raised our hands. "I like candy, too," Brenda said.

"And cookies." Alex smacked his lips.

"Well, there won't be any treats today if you don't start playing better," Mr. Wrightman said.

"No treats?" Danny's jaw dropped open.

"This team isn't making good passes. You're not concentrating. You're not *thinking*." Mr. Wrightman smacked his fist into his palm. "I expect you to *win*. No more silliness. No more fun and games. I've taught you a lot. Now go out there and show me what you can do!"

"But Mr. Wrightman—" Brenda tugged at his sleeve.

"No excuses!" Mr. Wrightman raised his voice. "Real soccer players try to win."

"But—" Brenda begged.

Mr. Wrightman glared at her. "Eat your apples," he said.

I sat down to eat my apple slices. We were all very quiet. Lucy didn't try to stand on her soccer ball. Mitchell didn't pretend to communicate with the aliens by speaking into his shoe. And no one said, "I finished my snack! I'm the hero!" Not even Josh.

Instead, we all looked serious.

We didn't feel like the goofy Leftovers anymore.

Chapter 6

We tried to score lots more goals. We really did.

But soccer nets are pretty small.

"Keep running!" Mr. Wrightman shouted from the bench. I could see him pacing up and down behind the white out-of-bounds line. "Steal that ball!"

Mitchell had a determined look on his face. He slid onto the grass and tried to kick the ball away from an Angel. But he couldn't do it. And his shoe fell off, too.

"Try harder!" Mr. Wrightman slammed his notebook down on the bench.

I frowned. Anyone could see that Mitchell was trying hard.

Danny got the ball and kicked it out of bounds.

"Pass it!" Mr. Wrightman shouted. "Don't kick it out of bounds! Pass the ball!"

Danny looked at the ground. "This isn't any fun," he muttered.

"Catherine?" I heard Alex's voice from behind me. He looked scared. "I'm worried. If I let two more goals in, then nobody will get a treat."

"Just play as close to the goal as you can," I told him.

"Close to the goal," Alex mumbled. He nodded.

With ten minutes left in the game, the Angels still hadn't scored again. But neither had we. "Let's go!" shouted Mr. Wrightman. "Score some goals!"

"Goal, goal, goal!" Next to the bench, Lucy's sister Ava was picking up grass and throwing it all over the place. "Goal!" she shouted again.

"Not like that, silly," Sara told her. She pointed to the field. "See the ball?"

"Ball," Ava agreed. She stretched out her arms. "*My* ball."

The Angels kicked the ball toward our goal. One of their players dribbled past Lucy. Then she dribbled past Josh. When I ran to stop her, she dribbled past me, too.

Only Alex was left between her and the goal. "Get the ball, Alex!" I shouted. I turned around. But Alex wasn't coming out to get the ball. Instead, he was backing up.

Boom! The Angel player kicked it hard and straight. Alex bumped into the back of the net. The ball sped toward him. Carefully, slowly, Alex opened his arms and caught it against his chest.

"Oof!" He gasped for breath and staggered back against the rope.

"Nice catch, Alex!" I yelled.

"Goal!" the referee shouted.

GOOOOOAAAALL!

Goal? I thought. How could there be a goal? Alex had stopped the ball!

Alex looked confused. "But—" He held out the ball to show that he had it.

The referee grinned. "You made a nice catch," she said. "But you were standing in the goal. The ball crossed the goal line. So it counts. Three to two, Rangers."

"Oh." Alex looked as if he was about to cry.

I slapped my forehead in disgust. It was my fault, I realized. I had told him to play farther back. "As close to the goal as you can"—that's what I'd said.

Mr. Wrightman came running across

the field. "What happened, Slavik?" he shouted. "You let me down! And your whole team, too!"

Alex hung his head. He didn't look Mr. Wrightman in the eye.

I wanted to protect Alex. I felt like telling Mr. Wrightman that Alex hadn't let us down at all. He'd tried hard. He'd been playing that far back only because he was scared to let in any more goals.

But I didn't.

"All right. Three to two. Last chance for those Popsicles, team!" Mr. Wrightman told us. His voice was calm. But his eyes were steely.

"Poppacles!" Ava shouted. She pointed to the field again. "Where my ball?"

Danny kicked off to Josh. Josh passed it to Mitchell. Mitchell looked around carefully and made a long, long pass. "Get it, Brenda!" I shouted. I jumped up and down. I could see Brenda sprinting after the ball near the white lines. No Angel players were anywhere near. "Score a goal!" I yelled.

And then, suddenly, I saw something else.

Ava.

She was running onto the field with Sara behind her. "My ball!" she cried. She reached out in front of her. "My ball!"

I gasped. Brenda was running right in her direction! "Look out!" I yelled.

"Help!" Brenda dived to the side, barely missing Ava. She turned a somersault and sat up—just in time to see the ball roll out of bounds.

The referee's whistle blew. "Angels get the ball!"

"No! *My* ball!" Little Ava glared up at the referee.

It was pretty silly, and I started to laugh. So did Brenda. Even Alex was

snickering behind me. But Mr. Wrightman didn't think it was so funny. His
voice boomed out across the field.

"Get that baby out of here!" he
yelled. I could see the veins in his neck
sticking out. "That stupid kid just cost
us a goal!"

Stupid kid? I was shocked. "She's
just a baby, Mr. Wrightman," I wanted
to say. But I didn't dare. I'd never seen
Mr. Wrightman look so angry.

"Ava want ball," Ava said. She stuck
out her lower lip.

Mr. Wrightman crossed the field in
ten giant steps. "Don't you ever do
that again!" he yelled, and he swooped
down to pick Ava up.

"I'm sorry," Sara said. "I tried to
stop her."

"I don't care what you *tried* to do!"
Mr. Wrightman snapped. He set Ava
down on the bench. "Now stay there!"
he told her.

Ava took one look at him and began to cry.

And I almost felt like crying myself.

It was one thing when Mr. Wrightman snarled at us.

But who needed a coach who yelled at babies?

Ava didn't stop crying, either. And Mr. Wrightman just got madder and madder—mostly at us. When Lucy turned a cartwheel instead of chasing the ball, he stormed onto the field and took her out of the game. Lucy had tears in her eyes when she got to the bench. Then Mr. Wrightman benched Mitchell, too, when Mitchell's shoe flew off again. And finally he benched Matt because Matt pulled his arms into his shirt and turned it backward.

Missing all those players made it hard to keep up with the other team. We did our best, but the Angels had the ball most of the time. With two minutes to go, they scored again. The game was tied.

"Come on, Rangers!" Mr. Wrightman's face was purple.

I took a deep breath and kicked off. I was so tired from running, I was glad the game would end soon. I almost didn't care who won.

My pass went to Adam. But Adam was exhausted, too. He tried to kick the ball—and he missed. One of the Angels got it instead. She dribbled down the field with two of her teammates. Passing back and forth, they got past Josh—and past Alex.

"Goal!" the referee cried. The game was over.

I didn't look at Mr. Wrightman.

But Lucy told me later that he stamped the ground so hard, she thought his shoe would sink all the way to the middle of the earth.

Chapter 7

"Antler!" Mr. Wrightman was shouting. "Get the ball!"

The ball was spinning toward me, faster and faster. I gulped. I didn't see how I could stop it. But there wasn't any goalie behind me. Alex was hiding in the net so Mr. Wrightman wouldn't see him.

I was the only one who could keep the ball out of the goal.

But I was also the only one who could keep Ava off the field.

"Antler!" Mr. Wrightman roared. And suddenly I saw that the ball wasn't an ordinary soccer ball. It had Mr. Wrightman's face on it! I screamed and turned to run.

"Antler! Catherine Antler!"

I opened my eyes and looked around. I was in my own room, with the sunlight streaming through the windows.

I'm home, I thought. And it's morning. It was just a dream. I took a deep breath.

"Catherine! You'll be late for school!"

It was my mom's voice. "Coming!" I shouted, getting dressed as quickly as I could.

At lunch I sat with Lucy, Matt, and Joanna in the cafeteria. I didn't eat much. I had a knot in my stomach from worrying about our soccer game that afternoon. "I wish—" I began.

"You wish what?" Joanna asked.

"I wish my mom was still our soccer

coach," I said. Then I turned red because I'd just remembered that Mr. Wrightman was Joanna's father. "I mean—" I began.

Joanna nodded. "I know what you mean," she said with a sigh. "My dad can be a very nice dad. But he wasn't very nice to Lucy's little sister."

"He was mad because Brenda could have scored," I said. "That's no reason to yell at a baby."

"Mr. Wrightman isn't any fun," Matt said with his mouth full. "I think it's fun to put your shirt on backward. Sometimes it's more fun to put your shirt on backward than to play soccer."

"Cartwheels, too," Lucy added. "I don't think you should get benched for doing cartwheels. Especially if you only do a few of them every game."

"I don't know if I want to play today," Matt said. "Today I might want to be a worm and squirm around the field. I don't think Mr. Wrightman would like that. Maybe I'll just stay home."

"Hey!" I said. "We could all stay home!"

"Hey, yeah!" Lucy said. She stood up and did a little dance. "If none of us shows up, then Joanna's dad would have to play all by himself!"

I grinned. I could just see Joanna's dad playing against the Twins. "Do you think he'd bench himself if his shoe came off?" I asked.

Joanna shook her head. "His shoe would never come off."

"Oh." I felt disappointed. But I could feel another plan forming in the back of my mind. A better plan. We'd be at the game, but—

Suddenly I jumped up from my seat. "I've got it!" I whooped.

* * *

We all got to the field early that afternoon. "I don't understand why you wore a sweatshirt today," Mom said with a sigh. She had on a T-shirt. "All the kids are wearing sweatshirts," she pointed out. "Is this a new fad or what?"

"Not exactly," I said. I tried not to grin.

Mr. Wrightman still looked mad about the previous day's game. First he lined us up in the middle of the field and made us do jumping jacks. Then we ran laps—twelve of them! By the time we were done, my legs were aching and I was sweaty all over. But I didn't take off my sweatshirt.

"Yesterday wasn't a lot of fun, was it?" Mr. Wrightman asked.

For a moment I thought he was going to say he was sorry. That would be good, I thought. He could apologize to us. But mostly I wished he would apologize to—

"I'm your coach," Mr. Wrightman went on. He thumped his chest. "And that means I'm the boss. That means you have to listen to me. All the time!"

I sighed. He wasn't going to apologize after all.

"I expect you to come ready to play," Mr. Wrightman said. "There's no excuse for wearing your uniform shirt backward." He rolled his eyes at Matt. Then he glared at Mitchell. "Or for letting your shoe fall off in the middle of a game."

Matt nodded at me. "Time out!" he yelled. That was our signal!

"What's going on?" Mr. Wrightman's face was bright red.

I pulled off my sweatshirt and threw it on the grass. So did everybody else. I looked around happily.

Every single player had his or her uniform shirt on backward! Just like Matt's had been the day before.

Tweet! Mr. Wrightman blew a piercing blast on his whistle. "What is the meaning of this?" he shouted.

I looked at Mitchell. "Kick it!" he yelled. And one by one, we each kicked off our right shoe. We stood there on the field, grinning at Mr. Wrightman, with one shoe off and one shoe on. Just like Mitchell the day before.

Mr. Wrightman slammed down his notebook in disgust. "You kids are out of bounds!" he shouted.

Alex scratched his head.

"No, we aren't, Mr. Wrightman," he said slowly. "We're on the field. That means we're in bounds."

"I mean you've gone too far!" Mr. Wrightman yelled. "Everybody! Put your shoes on at once!"

My legs trembled. But I didn't reach for my shoe.

"And don't forget our secret weapon!" Lucy shouted. She clapped her hands. "Come here, Ava."

Ava laughed and toddled out to Lucy.

Mr. Wrightman clenched his fists. "I'm counting to three," he said in a low voice. "Anybody who isn't properly dressed by then is benched! Understand?"

One . . .

No one moved.

Two . . .

Still no one moved.

"I'll bench all of you," Mr. Wrightman threatened.

Brenda shrugged. "Then bench us," she said. "We don't want to play when we're being yelled at. So we just won't play at all. Unless you let us play with our shirts on backward."

"And with Ava," Lucy added.

"It's more fun playing with only one shoe," Danny chimed in. "And we'll do cartwheels, too."

Adam grinned. "I'll be goalie. I'll play *behind* the net. Won't that be cool?"

Mr. Wrightman looked around at us. "I—I don't believe this," he said at last. "You kids—" He shook his head.

We waited.

"I quit," Mr. Wrightman said. He took a deep breath. Then he walked over to the other end of the bench and sat down.

We looked at each other. Then we all looked at Mom.

"Mrs. Antler?" Danny asked shyly. "Would you be our coach again?"

Mom hesitated. "I don't know much about soccer," she reminded us.

"But you know about kids," Julie said.

"That's more important," Mitchell agreed.

"Please?" Brenda begged. Matt even got down on his knees.

Mom smiled. "All right," she said.

"Yes!" Brenda shouted. I slapped Mitchell five. Julie and Yin started dancing. Lucy and Matt did cartwheels, and Ava did, too. Sort of. And then we all put our shoes on again.

But we kept our shirts on backward.

Chapter 8

"So what are you going to remember out there?" Mom asked us with a smile. We put our hands over hers in the circle. The game was about to begin.

"Teamwork!" Julie cried.

"Play hard!" Brenda added.

"And have fun!" we all shouted. We lifted our hands up high. "Go, Rangers!"

GO RANGERS!!

We were pretty silly at first. Mitchell lost his shoe about ten times. Once Joanna pretended she couldn't see the ball, so she didn't score. Another time, Adam got down in the crab position and kicked the ball.

By the end of the first half, we were losing, 4–3. But we all laughed our way back to the bench. "Keep up the good work," Mom said, handing us our orange slices.

"First is the worst!" Julie yelled at Josh.

"No, I'm zero," Josh began. Then suddenly he grinned. "No, let's change it," he said. He pointed to himself. "First is the best."

"No fair," Julie said. She stuck out her lower lip.

"Wait till you hear all of it," Josh told her. He touched her on the shoulder. "First is the best. Second is the same."

Julie smiled. "I like that a lot better," she admitted.

"How about third?" Lucy wanted to know. "What's third?"

Josh thought a moment. "And third is the one with the awesome brain."

"That sounds nice," Mom told him. "You guys have played well so far. But I wonder if you can play even better. What do you think?"

"We can," we told her.

Lucy stood on her head next to the tree, trying to eat her orange slice upside down. "Maybe some cartwheels will help," she said.

Alex frowned. "Maybe I should build my wall again," he suggested.

"No." I shook my head. "No wall."

Suddenly Mr. Wrightman stepped forward. "I'm sorry," he told us in a husky voice. "I shouldn't have yelled at you. I might know a lot about soccer, but I don't know a lot about kids."

We all looked at the ground. I was glad he was sorry. But I didn't think we were the only ones he should be apologizing to.

"And I also want to apologize to Ava," Mr. Wrightman went on. He squatted in front of Lucy's sister and stuck out his hand. "I'm sorry."

That's more like it! I thought.

Ava looked at Mr. Wrightman. Then she slapped his hand. "Go, Wangers!" she shouted.

"Go, Wangers!" we all chimed in.

When the second half began, Adam kicked off. With the side of his foot! He passed to Brenda, who passed to Julie. Julie dribbled in and kicked the ball, but one of the Twins players blocked it. The ball bounced over the white lines. The referee blew his whistle.

"Julie?" Mom held out the ball. "Would you like to throw it in?"

"Me!" Yin came running up. "I'll throw it in," she said. She took a deep

70

Throw  In

breath and threw it right to Mitchell. He booted it as hard as he could. The ball sailed past the goalie and into the net—

And so did Mitchell's shoe!

His shoe hadn't been tied, I guess. But now the game was!

"Yay, Mitchell!" Mom shouted from the bench. Mr. Wrightman clapped, too.

"Does that count as two goals?" Alex asked me as Mitchell pumped his fist in the air.

"It should," I told him. "But it doesn't."

The Twins made some good shots, but Alex blocked them every time. He didn't even need a wall! He also remembered to stay out of the goal. "You're playing great, Alex!" Mom shouted.

With one minute to play, the game was still tied. "Score a goal!" Mom yelled. "Go, offense!"

I kicked the ball to Josh. He kicked it to Danny. Danny stopped it with his foot. I thought for sure he would kick it out of bounds, but he didn't. Instead, he passed it to Joanna. Joanna gave it a hard kick—right toward the goal.

Right near Lucy—

Who was doing cartwheels instead of watching the game!

"Lucy!" I yelled. But she didn't hear me.

The Twins goalie dived and knocked the ball off to the side. It curved through the air and came down right at Lucy. I held my breath. It looked like it would hit her right in the face.

But it didn't.

Lucy started one more cartwheel. Her legs spun up, up, up. Her foot soared into the sky—and hit the ball.

Whap!

The ball bounced against the ground and rolled into the net.

The referee blew his whistle. "Goal!" he shouted. "Rangers win!"

An upside-down goal! We all jumped up and down, even Mom. Then we ran down the field to congratulate Lucy.

"Hi, guys!" Lucy said from inside the net. "Wasn't that a great goal? Come on in! I'm pretending this is my house, and you can all visit me."

We looked at each other.

Lucy stuck her arm through a hole in

the net. "We can all get tangled up, just like spiders and flies."

I grinned at Joanna. She grinned back at me. Then the whole team ran forward to get tangled inside the net.

Even Mom.

by Tristan Howard

Don't be left out!

The Leftovers are the wackiest team in any league. No matter what the sport, fun and laughs are always part of the game plan.

BASEBALL:

☐ BBS56923-6 **The Leftovers #1: Strike Out!** $2.99

☐ BBS56924-4 **The Leftovers #2: Catch Flies!** $2.99

SOCCER:

☐ BBS89896-5 **The Leftovers #3: Use Their Heads!** $2.99

☐ BBS92133-9 **The Leftovers #4: Reach Their Goal!** $2.99

Available wherever you buy books or use this order form.

Send orders to:
Scholastic Inc., P.O. Box 7502, 2931 East McCarty Street, Jefferson City, MO 65102

Please send me the books I have checked above. I am enclosing $_____ (please add $2.00 to cover shipping and handling). Send check or money order—no cash or C.O.D.s please.

Name_____**Birthdate**_____

Address_____

City_____**State**_____**Zip**_____

Please allow four to six weeks for delivery. Offer good in U.S. only. Sorry mail orders are not available to residents of Canada. Prices subject to change.

LO496

THE WEIRD ZONE

#4

BIZARRE
EERIE
HILARIOUS

Written and Directed by Tony Abbott

It's a lump.
No, it's a bump.
No, it's a bunch of big
bad alien moles! These furry
invaders are out to do some damage
to the town of Grover's Mill. Will Jeff and
his friends be able to figure out what's up under
ground before these tunneling terrors take over?

Attack of the Alien Mole Invaders!

THE WEIRD ZONE #4
by Tony Abbott

WZ396